Postman Pat's
Cat-up-a-Tree
Party

Story by **John Cunliffe**   Pictures by **Joan Hickson**
From the original Television designs by **Ivor Wood**

Scholastic Children's Books,
Scholastic Publications Ltd,
7-9 Pratt Street, London NW1 0AE, UK

Scholastic Inc.,
730 Broadway, New York, NY 10003, USA

Scholastic Canada Ltd,
123 Newkirk Road, Richmond Hill,
Ontario, Canada L4C 3G5

Ashton Scholastic Pty Ltd,
PO Box 579, Gosford, New South Wales,
Australia

Ashton Scholastic Ltd,
Private Bag 1, Penrose, Auckland,
New Zealand

First published in the UK by Scholastic Publications Ltd, 1989
This edition published 1993
Text copyright © John Cunliffe 1989 and 1993
Illustrations copyright © Scholastic Publications Ltd and Woodland
Animations Limited, 1989

A longer version of this story has been previously published as
a Handy Hippo

ISBN: 0 590 54143 9

10 9 8 7 6 5 4 3

Printed in Hong Kong by Paramount Printing Group Ltd.

It was a sunny day in spring. They were all
in the garden. Pat was having a cup of tea.
Julian was playing on his bike, and Sara was
mending a puncture.

"Miaow! Miaow!"

That must be Jess. But where was he? Pat looked everywhere, but he couldn't see Jess.

"Miaow! Miaow!"

"Jess! Jess!" Pat called. "Can anybody see Jess? I can hear him, but I can't see him."

"Miaow! Miaow!" went Jess, and they all looked for him.

4

"He's up there," said Julian.

"Where?" said Pat.

"In the sky," said Julian.

"He must be flying after the birds," said Sara, "look, there he is!"

High up in the fir tree, they could just see Jess clinging to a branch.

"Jess, what are you doing up there?"
said Pat. "Are you playing at being a
squirrel? Come on down, and you can have
a saucer of cream."

But Jess stayed where he was, and
miaouwed... so sadly.

"Poor, Jess," said Julian. "What's
wrong?"

"I don't think he *can* get down," said
Sara. "I think he's stuck."

"Can you climb up and bring him
down?" said Julian.

Pat tried to climb the pine tree, but the branches were so close together that he couldn't even begin. And all the time Jess was miaowing that he wanted to come down.

Sara brought a chair out, and Pat stood on it and reached up for Jess; but Jess was too far away. Sara brought a table out. Pat put the chair on the table, and held everything steady, and Sara climbed up. The table began to wobble, and Sara grabbed at the tree, and made the tree shake. Jess went further up the tree.

Sara jumped down, and now she went all wobbly, and she had to sit down with a cup of tea till she felt better.

"We shouldn't climb up on chairs and tables," she said. "We could have a nasty accident."

"I don't know why he doesn't just turn round and come down backwards," said Pat.

"It's odd," said Sara. "Cats are marvellous at going up trees, but hopeless at coming down again. It just seems that they can't do it. It's a wonder that all the trees aren't full of cats."

Dr Gilbertson stopped to see what they were all doing.

"What are we going to do," said Pat, "about getting Jess down? He can't stay up there for ever."

"I'll soon think of a remedy," said the doctor. "Now, let's see. I'll need a box, a long stick, some string, nails, and some cat food."

"Now I think I can lay my hands on a good long stick," said Pat, "and we have plenty of boxes, and string..."

Dr Gilbertson fixed the box to the end
of the stick, and put some cat food in it.

"There you are," she said, "that should
do it. The patient should be down and
about in no time at all. All we have to do is
to hold the box up on the end of the stick.
Jess will smell the food, jump into the box,
and we will lower him safely to the
ground."

Dr Gilbertson poked the box up into
the tree. Jess looked at it, miaowed, but did
not move.

"You try, Pat," said the doctor.

Pat pushed the box high into the tree,
and they all talked to Jess.

"Come on, Jess. Come on, puss. Get in
the box, Jess. You'll be all right. Come on,
then, Jess."

Jess did not move.

11

The Reverend Timms called with the Parish Magazine.

"Are you having a garden party?" said the Reverend. "What's Jess doing up there?"

"Just sitting there," said Sara. "You could call it a cat-up-a-tree party. A new kind. You see, Reverend, Jess is stuck up the tree. The doctor kindly stopped to help, but her idea isn't working. Jess just won't get in the box."

"Well, no, I don't think I'd get in a box on the end of a stick if I were Jess," said the Reverend. "Would you? I'm afraid the Bible says little about cats, and nothing, as far as I know about cats in trees."

Now there was the sound of a tractor. It was Peter Fogg. He stopped to join in. They told him about Jess, and he had a good look.

"Come down, you silly cat," he said, but it did no good. "I know," he said, "I'll get him down with my tractor."

"How?" said Sara.

"It should be easy," said Peter. "I'll put my digger as high as it can go, then drive up to your hedge with the bucket as near to that tree as I can get it. Then Jess can jump in, and I can lower him to the ground."

"He wouldn't jump into a box on the end of a stick," said Dr Gilbertson. "And how's that cough of yours?"

"Oh, a lot better, thanks, doctor," said Peter. "But a tractor-bucket's different from a box. It's a lot bigger, for one thing."

"It's worth a try, I suppose," said the doctor. "Stand back everybody. We're going to try again."

There was a roar as the tractor started up, and they all saw the large bucket coming over the hedge. Jess had such a fright when he saw it that he went still further up the tree! Pat shouted, "Stop, Peter, stop!"

But the engine was making such a noise that Peter didn't hear him. There was a great crunching and grinding sound, and the tractor came right through the hedge. Oh dear, what a mess there was!

"What happened?" shouted Sara.

"Ooh, I am sorry," said Peter. "I was so busy watching Jess and the tree that I forgot there was a hedge in the way."

Just then, Mrs Pottage and the twins came along.

"Don't worry about the hedge," said Mrs Pottage. "We have plenty of spare fence-posts in our barn. Peter can bring some round tomorrow and mend that hole."

The cat-in-the-tree party was getting bigger and bigger. Mrs Goggins came next, then Alf and Dorothy Thompson. Pat dashed indoors to get the best tea-service out, and Sara brewed more tea.

Julian brought out the sugar-basin, and Katy and Tom helped him to hand biscuits round.

George Lancaster came with two dozen
eggs, and Miss Hubbard, passing on the way
to the church to arrange the flowers,
stopped to see what was going on. Not one
of them could think of a way of getting Jess
down from the tree.

"We'll soon have all Greendale in our garden," said Sara. "It's a good thing this doesn't happen every day. We'd never have enough biscuits to go round."

Then Ted arrived, and they were all talking at once, when Granny Dryden walked up the garden path. She banged her stick on the path, and stopped them all in their tracks.

"Whatever is going on?" she said.

"Well, it's Jess, you see..." Pat began.

"Do sit down and have a cup of tea and a cake," said Sara.

"Thank you very much," said Granny Dryden, "where is Jess? I haven't seen him today at all."

"Jess is up that tree," said Sara, "and he's stuck, and we've all been trying to get him down."

"Trying to get him down? Keeping him up more like! Poor Jess, up that tree all this time." Granny Dryden sounded cross.

"We've tried our best to get him down," said Pat. "Honestly, Granny Dryden, we have done our best. But Ted's going to get a ladder, and we'll soon have Jess down."

"That cat's too high for any ladder," said Granny Dryden. "But if you all do as I say, he'll soon be down. And you won't need any ladder."

"Can you get him down, Granny Dryden?" said Mrs Goggins, astonished.

"Of course I can," said Granny Dryden rather sharply. "I've seen cats in trees before any of you were born. It's an old tale, that one about cats not being able to get down from trees. It's just folks making a fuss and a stir that get them into a state, and they just won't come down, then. If you all go home and get your tea, Jess will come down in his own good time. You'll see."

"It's the wisdom of age," said the
Reverend Timms. "I think we should all try
taking Granny Dryden's advice. God works
in mysterious ways."

"It's just commonsense," said Granny
Dryden, "that's all. Away you go home,
every last one of you, and you'll see that I'm
right."

One by one, they all went home.

"I'll stay and help with the washing-up,"
said Granny Dryden. "You must have a
right bonny pile of it."

The birds didn't like it a bit,
having a cat in their tree. But it
was much quieter now that
everyone had gone, and Jess was
beginning to feel really hungry.
He thought he might just try his
claws to see if they would hold
him going backwards. He got
down one branch. There was
more tumbling in it than
climbing, and this was a very
scratchy tree. Down another
branch. Ouch! It was also a prickly
tree. Another branch. Slowly, very
slowly, Jess was working his way
down the tree.

In the house, Sara was saying, "I hope our Jess is all right. Do you think I should pop out and see how he's getting on?"

But Granny Dryden said, "Certainly not! He will get on much better without anyone fussing round him. You'll see. He's a clever cat. We had a cat like Jess when I was a young lass. It could have been his great-grandad. He was always going up trees. I remember once..." And Granny Dryden told them a story of long ago.

All this time, Julian was hiding behind the curtains, peeping out into the garden. He couldn't see Jess, but he could see the tree shaking as Jess tumbled his way down it. The shaking came closer and closer to the ground. At last, a very rumpled cat jumped from the lowest branch on to the grass, and ran to the house, to scratch at the door to be let in. And, oh what a fuss they all made of him!

"There you are!" said Granny Dryden. "I told you he'd do it! Good old Jess. Just like his great-grandad. *Clever* Jess."

Jess jumped on her knee, and she cuddled him and stroked him, and he soon began to purr.

"Look at his fur," said Pat. "He looks as though he's been through a hedge backwards!"

"He's done better," said Julian. "He's been through a *tree* backwards."

The tree had rubbed his fur the wrong way. It was sticking out in all directions, and it was full of pine-needles that itched and prickled.

"Oh, poor old Jess!" said Sara. "He looks like an unmade bed. He needs a good brushing. That'll get the needles out, and then he'll feel a lot better. Won't you, Jess?"

Jess didn't like being brushed, but it did get the needles out, and he did feel better. Well enough, indeed, to go looking for mice after tea in Mrs Pottage's barn. But it was a long time, a very long time, before he climbed a tree again.